This Book Belongs to:

....

Hugs from Pearl

story and pictures by Paul Schmid

HARPER

An Imprint of HarperCollinsPublishers

Pearl is sweet.

She goes to Wildwood School.

She's a very good friend to have.

She plays fair, shares her

lunch treats, and best of all . . .

Pearl LOVES to hug.

Hugs are nice.

EXCEPT when they come from
a porcupine. And do you know
what Pearl is?

Well, you already guessed that.

Everyone in Pearl's class
LIKED getting hugs from her—
they were just a little ouchy.

Pearl's teacher kept lots of
Band-Aids handy. Her classmates
were very nice about it, too.

But Pearl didn't WANT anyone to say "Ouch! Thanks, Pearl. Ouch!" when they got hugs.

So Pearl decided to do something about it.

She tried putting pincushions on her quills, but that took WAY too long. She couldn't reach most of her quills anyway.

Then Pearl took a long, long bath
but found her quills did not get
ANY softer.

Finally, Pearl begged her mom
to give her a quillcut. Her mom
explained that quills grow back.

Pearl was perhaps a little
discouraged.

"What's a friendly little porcupine to do?"
She sighed.

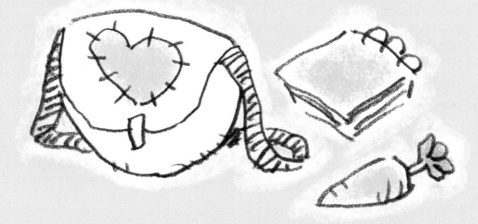

Pearl did not feel like giving
hugs that day at school.

On her way home, she stopped
to watch the rosebushes to see
how THEY handled things.

The bees buzzed happily among
the flowers. The bees skipped the thorns.

That gave Pearl an idea.

"Oh!" she squealed, and ran home.

Pearl dashed upstairs to her parents' bedroom. She grabbed one of her mom's special pillowcases.

The one decorated with all the roses.

She cut holes in the pretty fabric.

A snip here, here, and there.

Pearl smiled.

Then, without saying a word to anyone,
Pearl folded the pillowcase neatly
and put it in her schoolbag.

Pearl ran all the way
to school the next morning.

When the other children
arrived, there was Pearl
in her brand-new rose dress.

EVERYBODY got a hug.

Twice!

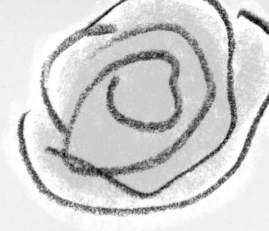

For Mr. Parks

Library of Congress Cataloging-in-Publication Data
Schmid, Paul.
  Hugs from Pearl / by Paul Schmid. — 1st ed.
    p. cm.
  Summary: A friendly porcupine figures out how to give hugs without hurting others with her sharp quills.
  ISBN 978-0-06-180434-2 (trade bdg.) — ISBN 978-0-06-180433-5 (lib. bdg.)
  [1. Porcupines—Fiction. 2. Hugging—Fiction. 3. Schools—Fiction.] I. Title.
PZ7.S3492Hu 2011   2010015906
[E]—dc22   CIP
                                                                           AC

Typography by Dana Fritts
11 12 13 14 15   SCP   10 9 8 7 6 5 4 3 2 1 ❖ First Edition